For James

WITH SPECIAL THANKS TO:

Suzanne Carnell, Chris Inns, Jo Spooner,
Helen Weir, Jenny Shone, Emma Farrarons

Starbird

Sharon King-Chai

TWO HOOTS

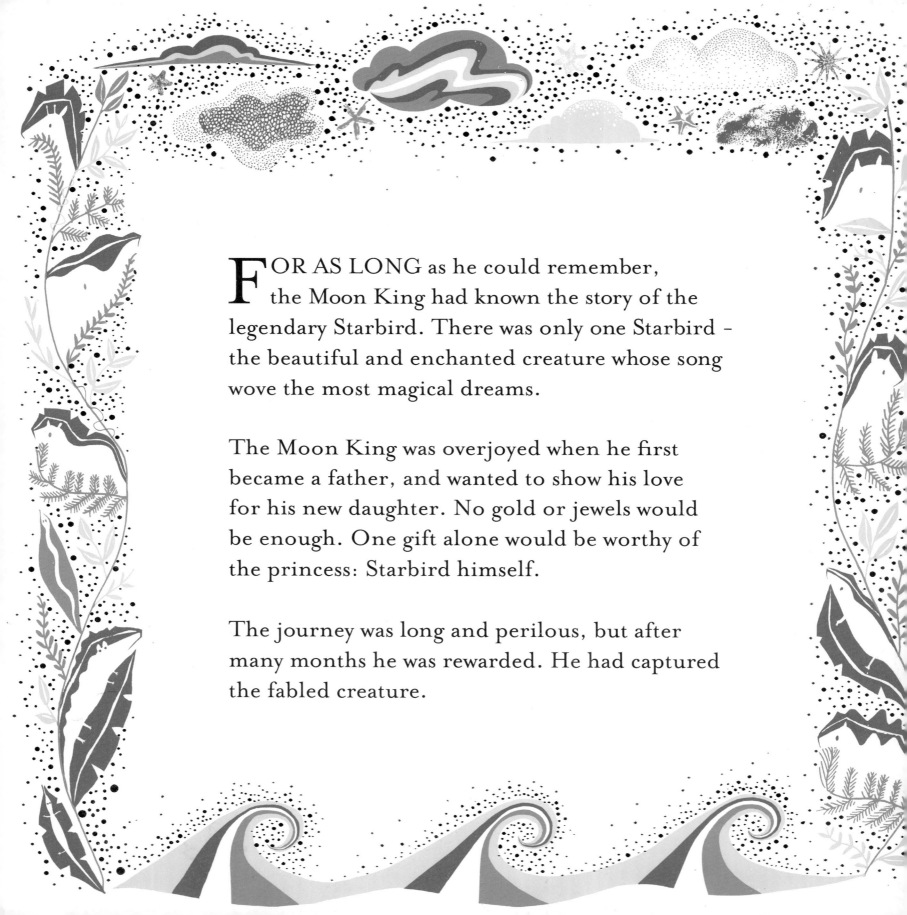

FOR AS LONG as he could remember, the Moon King had known the story of the legendary Starbird. There was only one Starbird - the beautiful and enchanted creature whose song wove the most magical dreams.

The Moon King was overjoyed when he first became a father, and wanted to show his love for his new daughter. No gold or jewels would be enough. One gift alone would be worthy of the princess: Starbird himself.

The journey was long and perilous, but after many months he was rewarded. He had captured the fabled creature.

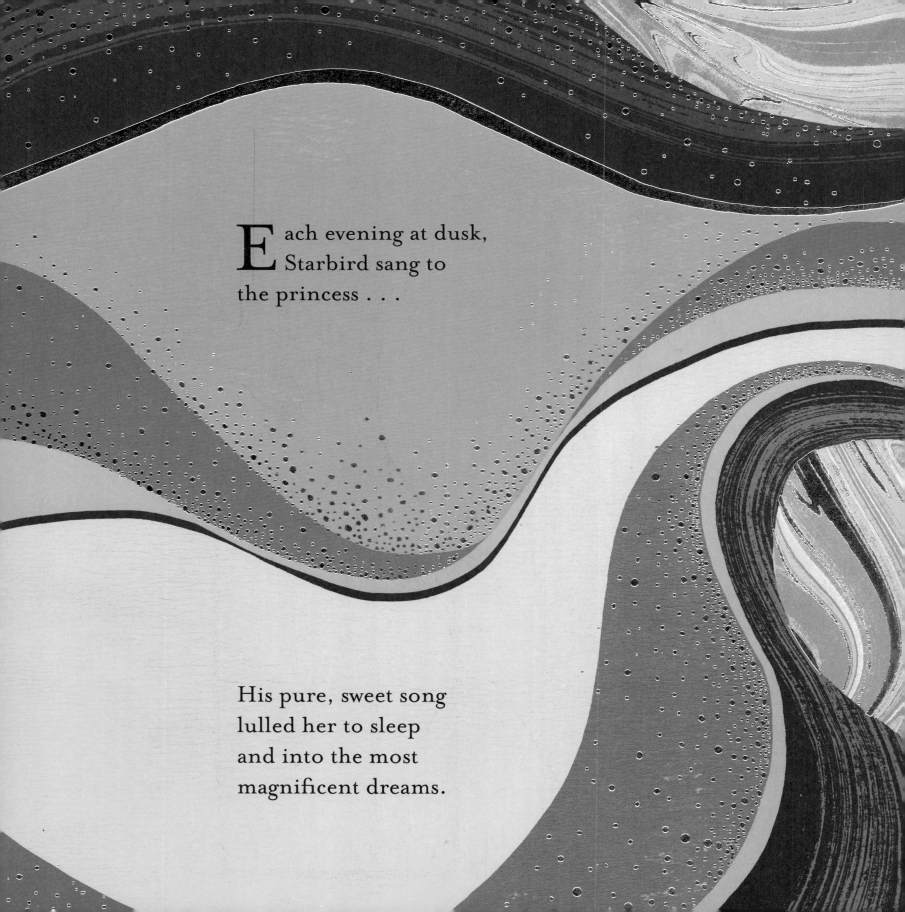

Each evening at dusk, Starbird sang to the princess . . .

His pure, sweet song lulled her to sleep and into the most magnificent dreams.

One day, she noticed
a sadness colouring
Starbird's voice.
She could not bear
to see him unhappy.

The princess opened
the cage door:
"Go, be free, Starbird!"

He spread his wings wide with joy. Free at last, Starbird soared higher
and higher into the sky, away from the castle and out of sight.

When he learnt
what the princess
had done, the
Moon King flew
into a rage.

How could his beloved
daughter reject the gift
he had risked so much
to bring her?

Angrily he vowed to search
the globe until he found
Starbird and returned
him to the castle.

By day, the Moon King slept, and Starbird
could fly freely in search of his home.

But as day turned to dusk, the first star of
the night appeared and warned Starbird
to hide before the Moon King awoke.

With a flutter of thanks, he swooped down to the jungle world below him.

Here he
befriended all the
creatures, who
were enchanted
by his songs.

As the dark cloak of night descended, the stars and his new jungle friends helped Starbird hide, safe from the Moon King's piercing gaze.

But the jungle was not home, and when morning came, Starbird set off once again. He flew so far and low, the land turned liquid.

Whoosh! The cold water engulfed him as he entered the underwater wonderland.

The sea creatures were
fascinated by him and that
night kept him hidden from
the omnipresent Moon King.

But Starbird knew he did not belong in the sea. When the sun rose he flew far, until the ocean below turned dry and dusty.

In the desert, the heat was strong, but the animals showed him where to find shade, and water to drink.

As night fell, they clustered under the sprinkling of stars, hiding Starbird in the vast landscape.

The next day Starbird
flew higher and
higher, to where the
tops of the mountains
scraped the sky, and
animals lived among
the clouds.

He revelled in
the freshness
of the cool air
— surely he
would find
his home
soon.

As the sun retired in deep dark shadows, the mountain creatures told Starbird of a faraway land where the birds sing together and make homes in trees as old as time itself.

With hope and
happiness in his song,
Starbird woke before
dawn. Perhaps he didn't
notice that the stars were
still gently twinkling.
Perhaps he didn't see the
Moon King hiding in
the shadows . . .

As he took flight, the Moon King pounced.
Starbird was prisoner once again.

The Moon King gleefully returned the caged bird to the castle.

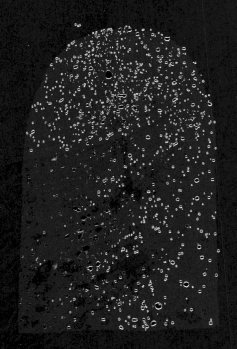

But life behind bars was no life at all. Starbird could no longer live this way. He could not eat or drink, he could not even sing. Starbird sat silent in his cage, defeated.

The princess dared
not defy her father
again by opening the
cage, but she begged
the Moon King:

"Father, Starbird doesn't
belong here. Please, he
can't sing any more!"

"Nonsense!" her father said.
"He will sing again."

But he didn't
sing again.

As the days
passed,

Starbird grew
thinner and
thinner,

sadder and
sadder.

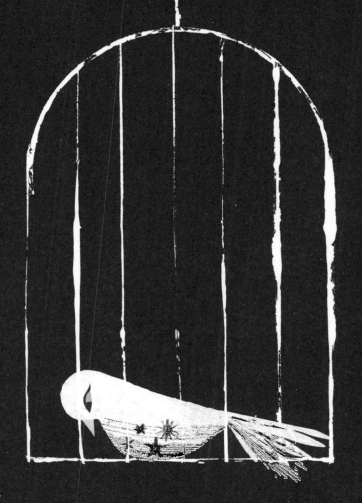

The princess pleaded with
her father once again:
"How can we be so cruel?
Starbird belongs in the sky.
Please, Father!"

The Moon
King looked
at the tears in
his daughter's
eyes, and looked
inside the cage
once more . . .

The next day, when the princess went to visit Starbird, the cage door was open.

A single feather lay on the floor, all that was left to show Starbird was once there.

The Moon King embraced his
daughter, his face salty with tears.
She knew he finally understood.

First published 2019 by Two Hoots
This edition published 2020 by Two Hoots
an imprint of Pan Macmillan
The Smithson, 6 Briset Street, London EC1M 5NR
Associated companies throughout the world
www.panmacmillan.com
ISBN 978-1-5098-9957-9

1 3 5 7 9 8 6 4 2
A CIP catalogue record for this book is available from the British Library.
Printed in China

The illustrations in this book were created using paint, ink, leaves,
potatoes, feathers, collage and Photoshop.
www.twohootsbooks.com